Danger at Sea

Written by Maria Grace Dateno, FSP
Illustrated by Paul Cunningham

Pauline
BOOKS & MEDIA
Boston

Library of Congress Cataloging-in-Publication Data

Dateno, Maria Grace.
  Danger at sea / written by Maria Grace Dateno, FSP ; illustrated by
Paul Cunningham.
      pages cm. -- (Gospel time trekkers ; [3])
  Summary: In the third book of the series that follows the adventures
of three siblings as they travel back to Gospel times to find Jesus and
learn to discover him in their everyday lives, Noah, Hannah, and Caleb
are transported to the village of Gennesaret, where they join a fishing
boat on the Sea of Galilee and meet Rebecca who had an encounter
with Jesus and his disciples.
  ISBN-13: 978-0-8198-1891-1
  ISBN-10: 0-8198-1891-7
  [1. Time travel--Fiction. 2. Brothers and sisters--Fiction. 3. Jesus Christ-
-Fiction. 4. Fishers--Fiction. 5. Christian life--Fiction.] I. Cunningham,
Paul (Paul David), 1972- illustrator. II. Title.
  PZ7.D2598Br 2013
  [Fic]--dc23
                              2012043606

Cover design by Mary Joseph Peterson, FSP
Cover art by Paul Cunningham

Published by Pauline Books & Media, 50 Saint Pauls Avenue, Boston,
MA 02130-3491

Printed in the U.S.A.

DAS KSEUSAHUDNHA6-91048 1891-7

www.pauline.org

Pauline Books & Media is the publishing house of the Daughters of St.
Paul, an international congregation of women religious serving the
Church with the communications media.

3 4 5 6 7 8 9   19 18 17 16 15

Dedicated to my niece and goddaughter, Bernadette, in the hope that she will do the same thing for me one day.

Contents

Chapter One

Weeds and More Weeds

It was a hot day late in June, and I wasn't planning on going outside that afternoon. But then I heard Dad talking to Mom in the kitchen.

"The weeds are getting pretty thick," he said. "Maybe the kids could do some work in the garden this afternoon."

My older sister Hannah, who had just turned eleven, was standing there in the living room too. We looked at each other. Neither of us likes weeding, so we quietly slipped out the front door.

As we snuck around the side of the house *opposite* the garden, we ran into my little brother, Noah. He looked all excited.

"Caleb! Hannah! I have an idea!" he said.

Noah is only six, so I wasn't expecting any really great idea from him. But anything was better than weeding.

"Okay, Noah," I said. "Let's hear it."

"I have an idea for how we can go there again!"

"Go where?" said Hannah. "Oh, never mind. I get it."

I got it, too. Noah was saying he had an idea for how we could go back in time. It might sound unbelievable, but it had happened twice before. Noah and Hannah and I went back to the time of Jesus and had great adventures! For weeks, we had been trying to figure out how to go there again.

The first time we had been riding our bikes down a hill. The second time we had jumped off a tree branch together. We had tried riding our bikes everywhere, and jumping off everything. (Except the roof. Dad wouldn't let us try that.) Nothing had worked. So I was willing to try anything, even one of Noah's ideas.

Hannah was, too.

"Okay, what's your idea?" she asked.

"I think we should try rolling down the hill together!" said Noah.

Hannah looked at the hill in our front yard. It's barely a hill, really, and not very steep.

"Well," she said, "I'm game."

"I guess it can't hurt to try," I said.

We lay down in a row and started rolling down the hill. Noah immediately banged into Hannah.

"Ow!" Hannah yelled. "Your foot!"

"Sorry!" said Noah.

It wasn't steep enough for us to really get going, though. We had to keep pushing off to keep rolling. I started laughing at how ridiculous we were. Soon all three of us were laughing. At the bottom of the hill, we sat up. Hannah's ponytail was lopsided. Noah's sand-colored hair had pieces of grass in it. I guess mine looked the same.

"Oh!" said Noah, looking disappointed. "We're still wearing our clothes!"

That made Hannah laugh even more.

"I should hope so!" she said.

What Noah meant was, we were still wearing the *same* clothes. When we went back in time, the way we could tell it happened was that our clothes turned into tunics, like they wore back in the time of Jesus.

At that moment, Mom stuck her head out the front door.

"What are you guys doing?" she asked.

"We're trying to go back in time," said Noah. "But it didn't work!"

That made me and Hannah laugh even harder!

"Well, if you have nothing better to do than roll down the hill, could you please go and do some weeding in the garden?"

"Ugh!" I said.

"Yuck!" said Noah.

"Oh, Mom!" said Hannah.

None of us liked weeding the garden.

"I did most of the work last time," I said. "I shouldn't have to do more."

"You did not!" said Hannah. "I did all the herbs. And I did all the squash and that's really prickly."

"I did all the tomatoes and beans," said Noah. "I did a lot for my age."

"I know you all worked hard before," said Mom, "but weeding a garden isn't something that you only do once. If the three of you work together, it won't take you that long. At least you can do a couple rows each." She went back inside.

"Well, she did say, 'if you have nothing better to do,'" I pointed out. "I can think of lots of things better to do than weed a garden. Like work on my Space Club project."

"I have a club project, too, Caleb!" said Noah.

"Well, I have other things to do, too," said Hannah. "Like the graphic design project Mom asked me to help with."

We all looked at each other. I knew we should go do what our mom asked, but I just really hated weeding.

"But Mom did ask us to do the weeding," said Noah.

"Yeah," said Hannah.

"Well, I guess we should," I said. We got up and headed toward the garden.

"But I don't want to do the Swiss chard and beets again," I said. "I'll do the squash. I can do it a lot faster than you, Hannah."

"I can do the beets," said Noah. "I'll do a better job than you, anyway, Caleb. You have to really get down and make sure you get the weeds close to the roots."

"I'll do the tomatoes," said Hannah. "They're easy. I don't know why you complained about them, Noah."

As she was talking, Hannah lifted the latch on the chicken wire fence around the garden. It's to keep out the deer and rabbits. We walked into the garden, and I bent down to pull some weeds at the beginning of the row of squash.

That's when it happened. I felt like the air became thick and I was moving in slow motion as I bent to the ground. A couple seconds later, I straightened up and looked down at my clothes. My shorts and tee shirt were gone, and I was wearing a long, light brown robe, tied with a belt.

Yes!

Chapter Two

Running into Rebecca

"Yay!" yelled Noah. "It happened! We're back!"

Hannah was laughing. "I can't believe it," she said. "After all those things we tried!"

"And we don't have to do the weeding!" I said.

"At least not for a few minutes!" said Hannah.

We all burst out laughing because technically that was true. The last two times we went back in time, we were there for two nights.

But when we ended up back home, only a few minutes had passed and no one had noticed we were gone.

"Look! There's water over there," said Noah.

"Maybe it's the Sea of Galilee," said Hannah. "So we're probably not in Bethlehem or Cana." Those were towns we had been to before.

"It looks like a lake to me," I said.

"The Sea of Galilee is a lake—a big lake," said Hannah. "It's just *called* a sea. It's also called Lake Gennesaret."

We could see the water between some houses. This town wasn't as big as the towns we had visited before. It seemed more like a bunch of houses on the edge of the lake.

We headed toward the water. Down the shore we could see some men and three or four boats. The boats were up on the beach and the men were doing something nearby. It seemed to be late afternoon.

We turned to look as some children came running out from between the houses and toward the water. There were six or seven of them—all younger than me. They seemed to be playing a game because one of them was being chased by the rest. She had something in her hands and the others were trying to get it. All of them were laughing and yelling as they ran.

The girl being chased ran right to the water and then turned to run along the shore, her bare feet sometimes splashing in the shallow water at the edge. One of the boys chasing her caught up as she turned. He reached out to grab the thing in her arms. It looked like a small pillow.

"Ha! I got it!"

"Aah!" she yelled as he took it and ran off, with the others now chasing him.

The girl stopped and leaned over to catch her breath. She saw us standing not far away.

"Oh! Hello there!" she said.

"Hello," Hannah answered.

"You're a fast runner," said Noah. "Almost as fast as me. Do you play on a soccer team?"

"On a what?" asked the girl.

"Nothing. Never mind. My name is Hannah," my sister said.

"I'm Caleb, and this is Noah. What's your name?"

"I'm Rebecca," the girl said. "I've never seen you here before. Are you travelers? When did you get here? Where are you from?"

"Well, we're kind of lost," I said. "What town is this?"

"This is Gennesaret! It's a village, really. A fishing village. You see those men getting the nets ready? That one standing there is my father. The other two are my oldest brothers. My other brother, Seth, usually goes to help, but he broke his leg and cannot go. He is not happy about having to stay home. And my father is not happy, either. But anyway, Seth is not yet strong enough to throw and haul the nets. He is younger than those two. He can only help to collect the fish and steady the torch."

This Rebecca seemed to like to talk a lot! When she finally paused to take a breath, I asked, "How old are you, and how old is your brother with the broken leg?"

"I am the youngest child, and I am almost eight. My two oldest brothers are all grown up already. One of them is married. My brother Seth, the one with the broken leg, is ten. You must be ten—you are as tall as he is."

"I'm nine," I admitted, straightening up a little. "But I can do a lot of things ten-year-olds can do. I could help your father on the boat. I could easily steady the torch and do whatever else Seth is supposed to do."

I was thinking that it would actually be a lot of fun to go out on a fishing boat.

"Caleb," said Hannah, "I don't know if that's a good idea."

"Why not? I can help. Maybe Rebecca's mother would let us stay with them."

"Well," said Hannah, "we do need a place to stay—"

"Oh, I think that would be good!" said Rebecca. "Father says that they have been missing Seth's help. They have not caught as many fish. They need to catch extra fish so that some can be dried. Without Seth to help take the fish out of the nets, they do not get as many. They only get enough to sell fresh and very little to be dried. And that makes Seth feel bad because it's his own fault he broke his leg. He was climbing the rocks. They set his leg and said he has to stay lying down for a long time so it can heal straight. He is angry that he can't get up. But my mother says that less fish is better than Seth being lame his whole life, and she will not let him go even though he says he could help sitting down in the boat. My father thinks—"

"Well," I said, interrupting her, "I like to go fishing, and I would be happy to help. I'm good at stuff like gathering fish. I could help throw the nets, too." Seth was probably small for his age and not as strong as me, so I was sure I could handle it.

"We use fishing rods when we go fishing," said Noah. "My dad has a new reel that he really likes."

"What?" asked Rebecca.

"Nothing. Never mind," I said. "Let's go talk to your father."

"Can I come help on the boat, too?" asked Noah.

"No, you are too small," said Rebecca. "Seth has been helping wash and mend the nets for years, but he was not allowed to go on the boat until last year. You look younger than me, so you are much too young, that is for certain."

"I'm six, but I can hold a torch, that is for certain."

"No, you will only be in the way. And you will fall asleep in the boat and fall overboard."

"I will not!" said Noah, getting angry.

"Noah, I need you to come with me to meet Rebecca's mother," said Hannah. "And we need to find out about you-know-who."

"What?" asked Noah.

"Who?" asked Rebecca.

"We were wondering if you had ever met a man named Jesus," said Hannah.

"Oh, yes, I know him," said Rebecca.

Chapter Three

A Job on a Boat

"You know Jesus?" I said. "Great!"

"Yay!" said Noah, forgetting about the fishing.

"Yes, he's the potter, and my friend Elizabeth is his daughter. She has three brothers and five sisters, and she is the youngest child, like me. She helps prepare the clay. It's fun to watch her father make the pots on his wheel and—"

"Wait a minute," said Hannah. "That can't be right!"

That's exactly what I was thinking. A potter? Jesus wasn't a potter. He was a carpenter. And he didn't have a daughter named Elizabeth!

"The Jesus we know is a traveling teacher," said Hannah. "He's from Nazareth, but he goes around teaching and healing. I thought maybe he had visited this village."

"Oh, *that* Jesus! Yes, of course," said Rebecca, laughing. "He has come here a few times with his disciples. We love when he comes—he is very nice to children. But most of the time you cannot get anywhere near him. Crowds of people, especially sick people, come to him. It is hard to get through and see him. But once he talked to me when I was visiting my aunt in Capernaum. That is a town very close to here. Jesus arrived at the town while I was there.

"I think Jesus will be coming to visit again soon," Rebecca continued. "I heard Abba and Imma talking about him."

We knew from our last trips that kids here called their dads "Abba." It seemed that "Imma" was what they called their moms.

"Let's go over and tell my father that you will come and help on the boat tonight. I am sure he will be glad. Like I said, he has been having a hard time since Seth—"

"Wait," I interrupted her again. "Did you say tonight? I was thinking that it would be tomorrow morning."

Rebecca laughed.

"Imagine thinking that you would be going fishing in the morning! I thought you said you liked to fish. What does your father do for a living?"

"He's a carpenter," I said, before Noah could say something confusing about selling toys online, like he did before. "He is teaching me how to make all kinds of neat things with wood."

"Oh, I can see why you would not know about fishing, then. The men of this village always go fishing at night. That way, the torch attracts the fish in the darkness and they come up toward the boat. They do the same thing in Capernaum, where I have an aunt. I do not know if that is how they do it in all villages—"

Rebecca kept talking all the way over to where her father and brothers were working. I stopped listening because I was looking around at everything. There were houses quite near the lake. At one house, I could see nets hanging over a wall. It seemed to have small metal things hanging from the edges. There were two other boats on the beach, besides the one we were walking toward.

Rebecca went up to her father and told him our names. She said that we were in town without any family and had no place to stay. He asked if our parents knew where we were, and we told him they wouldn't be worried. So he invited us to stay at his house.

"And Caleb says he will help on the boat, Abba!"

It turned out that Rebecca's father, Nathan, was not sure if he wanted my help. He asked what my father did for a living. I told him my father was a carpenter. But I said I was sure I could help with the torches and gathering the fish. I didn't say anything about the nets.

"But do you have good balance? And can you keep out of the way as we cast the nets?"

"Definitely!" I said. "I have very good balance, and I'm fast. I won't fall asleep or fall overboard."

Nathan laughed.

"Yes, all right," he said. "It has been slower without Seth. That boy had to go and break his leg at a most inconvenient time."

"I will bring Hannah and Noah to our house, Abba," said Rebecca. "And I will tell Imma about Caleb."

"Yes, bring them home and tell your mother to send enough breakfast down to the shore for all of us when we come in."

They went off, and Nathan showed me where I would sit in the boat and how to keep out of the way of the ones who were rowing. He definitely talked a lot less than his daughter.

"These are my sons: Joseph and Ezra." They each nodded as Nathan said their names. Joseph gave me a friendly smile.

Nathan said he'd light the torches when

they got out on the lake, and I needed to be ready to move them or hold them up when asked.

"What are those for?" I asked, pointing to some large open baskets that were in the boat.

"For the catch, of course," said Joseph.

Chapter Four

Fishing at Night

It was quite dark by the time we were ready to push off from the shore. But just then, Rebecca came running up.

"Abba, wait!" She had something in her hands.

"Imma says that this is for Caleb. It will be cold out on the water, and I told her he only had his mantle."

Joseph was still on the shore, ready to help push off, so he took what she had and passed it to me. It was like another tunic, but heavier and open in the front, like a coat. I put it on and tied it around me. It was nice and warm.

"Thank you, Rebecca," said her father. "Now run on home and tell your mother we are off and Caleb is warm."

Joseph pushed off from shore and jumped into the boat as Ezra pushed with his oar from the boat. Soon we were gliding through the water. There was a little light from the moon, but it was pretty dark. The men in the boat didn't talk at all, so neither did I. Joseph and Ezra rowed for quite a while, and then Nathan took Ezra's oar.

Once we got where they wanted to be, Nathan tapped me on the shoulder and pointed at one of the torches. I handed it to him and he lit it—I didn't see from what—and then I stuck it in the ring on the side of the boat that he had showed me before. We did the same with the other torch.

The torches were interesting—not like anything I had seen before. They were like a bundle of twigs, but the twigs were not what was burning. There was something stuffed in the middle of the bundle that was lit. It smoked a lot, too.

We waited a bit after lighting the torches, and then Ezra cast a net. He threw it really far, and now I could see why a kid wouldn't be able to do it. I felt a little embarrassed for telling Rebecca that I could.

A little later, they pulled the net in. The little metal things on the edge were weights. They sunk down and when the net was hauled in, the fish were caught in it. I was surprised to see a lot of fish. I tried to help grab them and put them in the baskets, but the first time I wasn't much help. The fish were still alive and kept flapping around. Grabbing them was harder than I expected.

The second time, I was more help, and I soon got the hang of it.

After a while, I started to get tired and had a hard time keeping my eyes open.

At one point, they rowed the boat over to another spot, and as we were going, my eyes started to close by themselves. I woke with a start when someone poked me, and I realized that the net was full of fish and I had to help.

That happened a couple of times, and then we started back in to shore. On the way back, the men talked and laughed together. They seemed happy about the catch, but I couldn't tell if I had made much difference. I was really looking forward to getting some sleep.

"Well, Abba," said Joseph as we got out of the boat and they started unloading the fish, "I think this boy is a good catch! He did well for his first time out, did he not?"

I smiled and turned to see what Nathan would say.

"Hmph. He did well, until he began to fall asleep. But let us see, tomorrow, after a good rest, whether he can keep awake."

"Seth will not be pleased about our taking Caleb, Abba," said Ezra. "He will think he is being replaced."

"Well, perhaps the son of a carpenter is lighter on his feet and will not be breaking his leg," said Nathan. He sounded annoyed, and I was proud of being able to help. I definitely wasn't going to fall asleep the next time.

Almost as soon as we finished unloading the boat, I looked up and saw Rebecca running toward us. She wasn't running as fast as when we saw her the day before, since she was carrying a large basket. But she looked very happy to see us.

"Good morning, Abba! Good morning, brothers and Caleb!" she said.

We each grabbed a small loaf of bread and ate it while standing around. I hadn't realized till I bit into the bread that I was starving!

The men started laying the nets out on the beach. Nathan said they would sort the catch and then wash the nets and lay them out to dry, but he sent me back to the house with Rebecca to get some sleep.

I barely remember the walk there, with Rebecca chattering constantly at my side. She showed me a place to lie down and gave me a blanket. I immediately fell fast asleep.

Chapter Five

Meeting Seth

When I woke up, it was bright daylight, and at first I couldn't remember where I was. Then it all came back, and I jumped out of bed. I went to find Hannah and Noah and see what was going on.

Outside, Hannah and Rebecca were chatting as they cut up some kind of fruit.

"Hannah!" I said as I ran over to them.

"Hi, Caleb," said Hannah. "How was your first night on a fishing boat?"

Rebecca handed me a piece of fruit—it was really good melon.

"Great! Exhausting!" I said with my mouth full. "Where's Noah? What have you all been doing? Have we found out anything about whether Jesus is around here?"

"Didn't you ask Nathan? Rebecca said he might know."

"No, there wasn't any chance to ask," I said, even though I hadn't remembered that Rebecca had said that.

"No chance? You were out on the boat for hours, waiting for fish to come. You had plenty of time," said Hannah.

"Hmph. That's what you think. Fishermen don't talk when they're out on the water. We don't want to scare the fish away, so we have to stay quiet."

"Well, anyway, the other fishermen are all still sleeping, so we will have to wait to find out if Nathan knows anything," said Hannah.

"Well, I could tell you what I know," said Rebecca. "I mean, I could tell you about when I went to stay with my aunt in Capernaum. I was helping her when she was sick. That's when I saw Jesus and he talked to me. It is a very good story. We need to find Noah so he can hear it, too."

"Oh yes, we can't have stories about Jesus without Noah," I said.

"He is cute, your little brother," said Rebecca. "I wish I had a little brother. I just have big brothers. When Joseph's wife has a baby soon, it will be like I have a little brother or sister, though too little to play with. Oh! Speaking of brothers, Seth has not heard this story yet. Let's go in where he is so he can hear it, too. He gets sad just lying there with his leg hurting."

I was looking forward to meeting Seth since he was close to my age. We went in the house and then out another door that went into a kind of courtyard. Seth was lying on a mat in the sun.

"Hi, Seth!" said Rebecca.

Seth looked over at us and frowned. He didn't look sad. He looked mad.

"Who are you?" he said, looking at me. "Your hair is strange looking."

"I'm Caleb," I said, trying to be nice, even though it was a mean thing for him to say.

"He is staying at our house, Seth. He is the brother of Hannah and Noah. He helped Abba last night."

"What do you mean he helped Abba?" asked Seth.

"He went out on the boat with them. He helped gather the fish and take care of the torches like you usually do. Since you could not go, he said he would go to help Abba in your place."

Seth frowned at me even more. "My father does not need another boy helping him on the boat. That is *my* job. Once my leg is healed, and it almost is, *I* will be helping on my family's fishing boat."

"I'm not taking your job!" I said. "I was just helping. You should be grateful instead of yelling at me."

"Just remember that it is not your place," said Seth.

"Well," I could not help adding, "your brother Joseph did say I was a good catch. I'll probably be helping to haul the nets tonight."

"Ha! That is not going to happen. You are too small," said Seth. "More likely, you will fall asleep and end up in the sea!"

"I'm not going to fall asleep," I said. "And I'm not going to fall overboard! I have good balance in a boat. *And* on the land."

Seth glared at me.

"So, Rebecca!" said Hannah. "Didn't you say you had a good story to tell us?"

Chapter Six

Rebecca's Story

"Yes," said Rebecca, "and Seth, you have not heard this, because it happened the week before you broke your leg, when I was gone helping Aunt Miriam in Capernaum."

"Well, it better be good. I need something to make me stop thinking about my leg," said Seth.

"Does it hurt a lot?" asked Hannah.

"A little," he said. "It's not that bad."

"It was in the afternoon," began Rebecca, "and I was out running an errand for Aunt Miriam. I was in another part of the town, where we have cousins. On the way back, I stopped at the potter's house. I like to watch potters. My friend Elizabeth's father is the potter here in Gennesaret. And then I went to pick some flowers for Aunt Miriam. I didn't mean to go far, but I wanted to get more of the little red flowers, so I went out along the road that comes into the town.

"I saw some travelers walking along, coming toward me, and I thought of running back home. But when they got a little closer, I could see that they weren't scary looking. I mean, they didn't look like robbers or anything. So I stayed there, picking flowers near the edge of the road.

"Anyway, the group of men passed by. One of them was walking a little in front. He looked like he was thinking. He saw me and looked over and smiled, but he did not stop or say anything. That was Jesus. Then the other men passed by. Those were his disciples. They did not even notice me. They were arguing among themselves. They sounded like my brothers when they are talking about who is the best fisherman."

"Ezra is the best," said Seth, immediately. "But when I am older, I am sure I will be. My father said I was the fastest of all his sons to learn how to mend the nets."

"I don't think you will ever be able to throw the net as far as Joseph can," I said. "He definitely throws it a lot farther than Ezra."

"That's not true!" said Seth. "Ezra throws farther, and his nets are better made, too."

I had no idea who made which nets, but I was just about to argue that Joseph did it better. Rebecca interrupted.

"That is a good example of what those men sounded like. I did not hear everything they were saying because they kept walking. But I could tell that they were all trying to show that they were the most important of the group."

"Did Jesus hear what they were saying?" I asked.

"It did not look like he was paying attention, but he actually was. As you will soon hear.

"They passed by, and I soon followed them because it was getting toward evening. I went home and Aunt Miriam told me to quickly take some of our fresh melons to Anna's house. She is the mother-in-law of one of Jesus's disciples. Jesus and his disciples stay at her house when they come to Capernaum. I do not know how my aunt had heard so quickly that they had arrived, but she wanted to give something for their supper.

"So I ran over to the house with the melons. When I went in, the men were in the court-yard. They had washed for the evening meal. As they came into the house, I heard Jesus say to the others, 'What were you talking about on the way here?'

"I gave the melons to Anna, who was pre-paring a meal for them. Then, instead of leav-ing, I went to stand in the doorway, because I wanted to hear what he would say to them. The disciples did not answer. They just looked embarrassed. So Jesus went and sat down on the floor and had them all sit down, too. And then, the most amazing thing happened. He looked over at me and he smiled. Then he went like this with his hand—" Rebecca made a "come here" motion with her hand.

"I suddenly felt very shy. I wanted to run out of the house, but he kept smiling and was waiting for me to come over. So, I walked over. He patted the floor next to him, so I sat down beside him. He looked at his disciples and said, 'Whoever wants to be first must be the last one of all. Whoever wants to be first must be the servant of all.'"

"That doesn't make sense," said Noah.

"Well, what he said next made sense. He put his arm around me and said, 'Whoever welcomes a child like this in my name welcomes me.' Then he smiled at me again. I will never forget that smile. It was like he was saying something to me . . . ."

Rebecca stopped talking and sat there staring, but not looking at anything. I could tell she was remembering Jesus smiling at her.

"And anyway," said Rebecca, coming back from her memory, "it does make sense. He was saying that we should not be fighting about who is best. We should be showing who is best by putting others first. Especially people who are younger or weaker than we are."

Chapter Seven

When Will Jesus Arrive?

"How can putting others first show who is best?" asked Seth.

I was thinking the same thing, but I didn't want to agree with Seth.

"I think," said Rebecca, "a really great fisherman can say nice things about how great the *other* fishermen are. He can say encouraging things to younger fishermen. A truly great fisherman does not need to brag about himself. That shows he is actually better than the ones who do, right?"

I could tell that Rebecca had been thinking about this a lot.

"Anyway, you can think about what it means for yourself. I just thought it was a good story."

It *was* a good story. Even though she seemed to use a lot more words than most people, Rebecca was fun to listen to. I think her brother thought so, too.

"Thanks, Rebecca," said Seth. He sounded quieter and less angry than when we came in. "It was nice of you to bring me some company and tell me stories."

"Is there anything I can get you, Seth?" she asked.

"No, I'm fine. You better get back to your chores. But maybe our guests can stay and talk?"

"Caleb has not eaten yet," said Rebecca. "And Hannah and I were helping Imma."

"Well, just Noah, then," said Seth. "Maybe you could stay for a while, Noah?"

We left the two of them talking and went to get me something to eat.

"That really was a good story, Rebecca," I said. "I wish I could see Jesus and hear him teach. We've been trying so hard to find him, but we never quite make it."

"Well, let's see if my father is up. We can ask him if there has been any news."

Rebecca's mother told us that Nathan was already out mending the nets.

We ran out to where the nets were spread out to dry. Rebecca's father and brothers had put them on some kind of wooden racks. Now they were checking for tears and mending the nets.

"Abba," said Rebecca, going up to her father. "Did you say that Jesus was going to be coming to our village soon?"

"Hm," said Nathan, not looking up from the mending. He had what looked like a large needle and he was carefully weaving a new thread into the net. "I think that's what I heard."

"Where did you hear it, Abba?"

He finally looked up from the net and saw me standing there with Rebecca. "Oh, so you are up now? How are you doing? Are you willing to come with us tonight?"

"Of course," I said, happy that he wanted me.

"I admit it is not polite of me to let a guest do work like this. But I will not hide from you that Seth's broken leg is like a broken leg for the whole family."

"I'm happy to help," I said. "But I was just wondering if you could tell me any more about when Jesus might come to this village. You see, my sister and brother and I really want to see him."

"I do not know for certain," he said. "All I heard is what is being said in the market. He is expected any day now."

"Any day now?" I said. "Oh, that would be fantastic! Maybe he will come while we're still here!"

Nathan went back to his mending. "You are welcome to stay as long as you like—until Jesus comes, certainly. If it is not in a few days, it will surely be within a few weeks."

A few weeks? Even if Nathan was willing for us to stay, I didn't think we would be there. The other two times we came back to the time of Jesus, it only lasted two nights. I really hoped Jesus was on his way!

Chapter Eight

Cold and Wet

That evening, I prepared to go out in the fishing boat again with Rebecca's father and brothers.

"We'll make you a fisherman yet, little carpenter!" teased Joseph as he gathered the nets to bring on board.

"It is getting windy, Abba," said Ezra. "Do you think it will be bad tonight?"

"Hm. Probably quite windy, but we will be fine. Bring a couple extra torches, in case we have trouble keeping them lit."

"The moon is almost full," said Joseph. "But the clouds are coming from the west, so we probably will not get much light. Maybe it would be better for Caleb not to come tonight."

"Why?" I asked. "I'll be fine." I didn't want them to think I was afraid of the wind and the dark.

"It's just that when it is extra windy and dark, things get a little more difficult. And you're just learning," said Joseph. "Even though you did a great job last night," he added.

Nathan paused and looked out to the water, then up at the sky.

"It will be fine, Joseph. He can come. Both of you just keep an eye on him."

"Sure," said Ezra.

"I will keep close to him," said Joseph.

"Yes, you keep close and we will catch as many fish as we can," said Nathan.

I had brought my outer mantle, and I could tell I would need it tonight. These fishermen dressed lightly so that they could move around. I had seen some of them on the beach with only a piece of cloth wrapped around their waists. But since I wasn't doing as much moving, I could wear more clothes and keep warm.

We rowed out to sea and I could definitely tell that it was windier than the night before. It was hard to get the torches lit. And one of them kept getting blown out.

"We will just use the one," Nathan said, speaking over the wind. We didn't really need to keep quiet this time. I'm sure the fish couldn't hear us over the noise of the waves and the wind blowing.

The first cast of the nets went well, and they hauled them in. The wind almost blew the basket out of Ezra's hands, but he grabbed it and we all helped to collect the fish. Then Joseph cast the nets. We waited, and then they hauled that catch in as well. I moved forward to help collect the fish . . . and that's when it happened.

I stood and leaned forward and a huge gust of wind came from the side. I lost my balance and fell. I landed against the stick of the torch, which gave way, and I fell into the water with it.

It happened so fast that I barely got out a yell, and then I was completely underwater. It was dark and very cold. But the scary thing was, I couldn't tell which way was up! I kicked my legs and waved my arms around and hit something with my hand. Wood. The bottom of the boat! Which way should I go? I couldn't hold my breath much longer.

I kept kicking my legs and tried to feel along the bottom of the boat, to get out from under it. I felt the curve of the boat and moved that way. Suddenly, a hand grabbed my wrist and pulled. As my head came out of the water and into the air, I took a huge breath. I had never been so happy to breathe!

"Hold still," said Joseph. "I have you. Stop kicking, and I will pull you up."

He pulled me into the boat, and I noticed that he was all wet, too. I immediately started shivering in the chilly wind.

"Did you fall in, too?" I asked him.

"No, Ezra held my legs so I could reach down and feel for you," he said. "You knocked the light out, you know."

I saw that Nathan was holding a newly lit torch.

"I'm sorry," I said, with my teeth chattering. "I lost my balance."

"You do not have much weight," Nathan said. "I should have listened to Joseph. He was right that it was too dangerous for you. Luckily, we got you back."

They made me take off my tunic and put on Ezra's. He was just wearing something wrapped around his waist.

"We should head back," said Joseph, and I noticed he was shivering, too.

"Yes, you and Ezra can row to keep warm. Caleb, sit way down over here so the wind will not find you."

We made it back and quickly went up to the house. Of course they weren't expecting us at that hour. I felt so bad that they would have almost no catch of fish and everyone would be woken up, all because of me.

Chapter Nine

Warm and Dry

"Nathan, what has happened?" I heard Rebecca's mother ask.

"Caleb fell in," said Nathan. "He is fine. Joseph reached in and pulled him out, but they both got chilled so we decided to call it a night."

"Ezra, get the fire going and warm some broth," I heard her say. "Where is Caleb? He should get warmed up quickly."

"I'm fine, thank you," I said, although I was still shivering.

"Here's a blanket," she said, and she wrapped it around me. She brought me over by the fire.

"What's going on?" I heard another voice ask. It was Rebecca.

"Go back to bed, Rebecca," said her father.

"But Abba, we can help. What happened?"

Ugh. How embarrassing. I heard him tell her, too, and she came over to where I was sitting near the fire. I saw that Hannah was with her.

"Are you all right, Caleb?" Hannah asked. She looked worried.

"I'm fine. I just fell in the lake and got wet. And it's windy so I got cold. I'm fine."

"Oh, I better go tell Seth what's going on," said Rebecca. "I am sure he's dying to know."

Oh, great. Now Seth would know he was right and I was wrong. I had said I wouldn't fall in, but I did.

I felt like hiding under the blanket, I was so embarrassed. Then Joseph came over, also wrapped in a blanket.

"So, are you warming up?" he asked. I nodded.

"This brings back memories, doesn't it, Abba?" said Joseph.

"Did you fall in when you were young?" asked Hannah.

"Me? No! It wasn't me," Joseph said, and he laughed.

"Was it Seth?" she whispered.

"No!" said Joseph, laughing again. "Seth has never fallen in," he added loudly, and I knew he meant for Seth to hear in the other room. "He is certainly destined to be a great fisherman, for he is more surefooted in a boat than when climbing rocks!

"No, it was Ezra," continued Joseph in a normal voice. "But it was kind of my fault. He was new and I was supposed to be working with him. My father had hired hands in those days, you see, before we, his sons, were old enough to be much use. I had bragged to Ezra that I got to haul the nets with the men."

"How old were you?" I asked.

"I was twelve or thirteen. Ezra was ten and had only been out at night a few times."

"How did he fall in?" asked Rebecca, who had come back from filling Seth in on things.

"Was it windy like tonight?" I asked.

"No," said Joseph. "No, it was a moonlit night, with little wind, although it was much colder. I was supposed to be with him, near the baskets. But I made my way over among the hired hands, to help haul in the nets. So, I actually did not see what happened, but it seems that one of the men, in pulling the nets, leaned back and knocked into Ezra. Ezra lost his balance, which is easy to do, and fell over."

"Poor Ezra!" said Rebecca. "Did you pull him out?"

"Abba reached over and grabbed his hair the moment he bobbed back to the surface. They pulled him on board, but, as I said, it was even colder, and he got very chilled. We hurried back, but it took hours to warm him up."

"Are you warmed up yet, Caleb?" asked Hannah.

"Yeah, I'm pretty warm now. Are you, Joseph?"

"Almost. I am just waiting for some hot broth to drink," he said, winking at Rebecca.

"Oh, I will go get it!"

"We got Ezra warmed up after a bit, and then the next night, I was much more careful of him on the boat," said Joseph.

I thought about being on the boat again the next night, and my stomach started to feel funny. I didn't think I wanted to go back out with the fishermen.

"Of course, Ezra was nervous about going out again after falling overboard. But there is one good thing about having a big brother," said Joseph.

"Oh, were you encouraging and told him not to worry?" asked Hannah.

"Ha! No, of course not!" laughed Joseph. "I can tell you do not have a big brother. He went because he did not want to act scared in front of me! I knew he was, of course, so I just confidently talked as if he certainly would be coming the next night. I didn't give him a chance to say he wasn't going to."

What Joseph said reminded me about when Noah was learning to ride a bike. He fell one time and scraped his leg badly. I could tell he didn't want to try again. But I think I just bragged about how I learned to ride a bike when I was even younger than he was. It did get him to try again, but probably I could have said something more helpful.

Chapter Ten

He's Coming!

We slept in, but not as late, since we had come home much earlier. When I got up and went outside, I saw Noah jumping around excitedly.

"Caleb! Caleb!"

"What's up, Noah?" I asked, rubbing my eyes.

"Caleb!" he said, still jumping up and down. "He's coming! He's coming!"

"Who?" I asked, still not quite awake.

"Jesus!" he yelled, still jumping. "Jeesuuss!"

"Oh! Jesus is coming? When? How do you know?"

"Oh, Caleb!" said Hannah, running over to us. "Did Noah tell you? We'll finally get to see him! Rebecca said that her mother heard at the market that he would be coming today!"

Rebecca went off with her mother to a neighbor's house, to help prepare a meal for Jesus. Her father and brothers were working on their nets as usual. We helped with a few chores, and before noon, Rebecca came running back into the courtyard.

"He is here! He is near the house of Samuel, another fisherman here in the village," she said, all out of breath. "It is down this street, the second to the last house by the water."

"Can we go see him now?" asked Hannah.

"I am!" said Rebecca. "I will go get my friend Elizabeth, and we will go together." She ran off.

Hannah and Noah and I looked at each other.

"It doesn't seem possible," I said.

"I know, but let's go see," said Hannah.

We had just started down the street, when I suddenly thought of something. Seth was in the house and probably didn't know yet that Jesus was here. We should probably go tell him.

The thing was, I really didn't want to talk to Seth. I didn't want him to say something about how I had bragged I wouldn't fall in the sea, but I did.

"Wait! We should go tell Seth," said Hannah. "I know he'd want to know."

"He can't get up and go see Jesus anyway," I said. "Why even tell him?"

"I'd want to know what's going on," said Noah. "Wouldn't you?"

"Yeah, I guess I would," I said.

We turned back and walked into the house. It seemed everyone else was gone.

"Hello!" we heard Seth calling. "Is anyone here?"

"Hi, Seth!" said Noah as we came into the room.

Seth was sitting up and had his good leg

swung over the edge of the bed, with that foot on the floor.

"What are you doing?" asked Hannah. "You can't put your weight on that leg. You'll ruin the healing that you've had so far."

"But where is everyone?" he asked.

"Jesus is in town!" said Noah. "People are going to see him. We just came back to let you know."

"Oh!" said Seth. "Where is he?"

"Rebecca said he was at the house of Samuel the fisherman," said Hannah.

"Oh," he said.

I was waiting for him to say something making fun of me for falling overboard, but he didn't. He just looked sad. I thought about how it must feel to be stuck in bed, especially when everyone else was going somewhere.

"Hey," I said. "Would you like us to get your brother Joseph? Maybe he could carry you to see Jesus."

"That would be great!" said Seth. "Thanks, Caleb." He looked down at the floor and then said more quietly, "And thanks for helping my father on the boat. You are doing a pretty good job for not having any experience in fishing."

"Not as good as you, I'm sure," I said. "I think you will be a great fisherman."

Seth and I smiled at each other.

"Okay, let's go tell Joseph, and we'll see you there, Seth," said Hannah.

We ran through the house into Joseph's. He was there with his wife, eating something.

"Joseph! Jesus is in town," I said. "Do you think you could carry Seth to go see him?"

"Certainly, I'll be right over to carry my clumsy little brother to see the teacher."

"Thanks!" said Noah, and we ran back through the house and out the door.

And that's when it happened. Right as we stepped out the door, the air was heavy and thick, and we were moving in slow motion. In a second, we were standing in our own yard, right in the middle of the garden.

"No!" I yelled. "It's not fair! We were so close to seeing Jesus."

Chapter Eleven

More and More Weeds

Noah sat down in the dirt. Hannah sighed.

"Oh well," she said. "We were closer this time. At least we were actually in the same town with Jesus."

"Yeah, this is the closest we've gotten," said Noah.

"That's true," I said. "Maybe next time!"

"What were we doing in the garden?" asked Noah. We all looked at each other, thinking.

"Oh, I remember! Mom asked us to pull weeds," I said.

We started pulling the weeds from among the plants. I went to the row of beans. Hannah was doing the row of lettuce, and Noah had sat down next to the tomato plants and was pulling the weeds that were growing right close to the stem.

As we worked, I was remembering what it was like to be on the fishing boat, catching the fish that we would eat the next day. We were doing kind of the same thing with our garden. I hadn't thought of it before. I had always just thought of planting, weeding, and watering as annoying chores. But it was neat to grow our own food like this. Even though vegetables were not my favorite thing to eat.

"Hey, Caleb," Noah said, interrupting my thoughts. "Maybe we could get Mom and Dad to grow some of those melons like Rebecca's family had growing in their courtyard. They tasted so good."

"I was wondering if we could get a fig tree," said Hannah. "Did you eat any of those fresh figs? They were great."

"Yeah, we can tell Mom and Dad that we

want to grow things in our garden like they used to grow in the time of Jesus!" I said.

"Maybe it will be more fun to weed the garden if we do," said Hannah.

We laughed and got back to work. We didn't stop until Mom called us for supper.

"Mom said you've been weeding. How far did you get?" Dad asked as we sat down for supper.

I was about to say that I had done a lot more than Noah—*all* the rows of beans, peppers, and lettuce. I stopped just in time, remembering Rebecca's story about Jesus. *Whoever wants to be first must be the last.*

"I think we just about finished," said Hannah. "Caleb really did a lot. Including the lettuce, which is tricky because it's easy to pull up the plant along with the weed."

"Noah was amazing," I said. "I've never seen such a weed-destroying machine before."

I looked at Noah, who was smiling really big.

"Oh, but Hannah did the most, Dad. She did all the squash, plus the spinach, and those other yucky green leaves."

Our parents were looking kind of puzzled.

"Well, that's great," said Dad. "I'm really impressed. Thank you so much for all your help."

"Mom, do you think we could grow melons next year?" asked Noah.

Chapter Twelve

All in the Same Boat

That Sunday when we went to church, two interesting things happened during Mass.

The first thing was when Father Joe read the Gospel reading. I couldn't believe it! The story was about Jesus in a boat with his disciples, during a storm. I could imagine so well what it was like! The wind and the waves would have been scary if the boat was filling up with water. The men must have been very afraid, even though some of them were fishermen and had been in a boat many times.

Jesus calmed everything down with three words. The wind stopped blowing and the waves stopped swamping the boat. No wonder the disciples were so amazed. Father Joe said that they were probably staring at him with their mouths open!

"But notice," he continued, "what Jesus was doing before he calmed the storm. It says he was lying there, asleep. As the storm arose and the waves started swamping the boat, Jesus was asleep."

I almost laughed out loud, remembering how I had fallen asleep in the boat, too.

"The disciples represent the Church," said Father Joe.

"We, the Church, are all in the boat with Jesus," he continued. "Even if there is a storm and we go through hard times, Jesus is with us. We have to do our best to work together because, as they say, we're all in the same boat!"

The second interesting thing that happened was that my family was asked to take up the gifts.

Every Sunday, the ushers choose a family to bring the bread and wine and the money that is collected up to the altar. It's called the "Preparation of the Gifts" because they are gifts we present to God. The bread and wine will become the Body and Blood of Christ that we receive in Holy Communion. The money is used for the Church and for poor people who need it.

Well, this Sunday, as we came in, before we walked up to the pew we usually sit in, I saw one of the ushers say something to my dad. He nodded his head, and then he told us that we had been asked.

"After the homily, we'll go to the back of the church," he said. "I'll tell you when."

I almost forgot about it during Father Joe's homily because I was interested in the boat story. But when we stood up to pray the Creed, Dad tapped me on the shoulder, and we all walked down the aisle to the back of the church.

We waited until everyone was singing, and then the usher handed my parents and Hannah the gold containers with bread in them.

There were two things left for me and Noah: the glass cruet of wine, and the basket with the money. It didn't really have all the money in it, just a little bit, to represent the rest.

I was sure the usher would give Noah the basket and me the wine, because when my friend Kevin's family brought up the gifts a few weeks ago, that's how they did it. He carried the cruet and his little sister carried the basket. Which makes sense because the basket isn't breakable.

So I was very surprised when the usher handed me the basket. I felt embarrassed and thought about what Kevin would say. He would brag that he got to carry the breakable thing and I had to carry the baby thing.

But there was nothing I could do because the server carrying the cross was there to lead us down the aisle.

It's not fair, I thought, imagining what Kevin would think as soon as he saw me.

But suddenly, as we walked down past all the people sitting in their pews, two things clicked together. I thought of Rebecca talking about the apostles arguing over who was most important. And I remembered Father Joe saying that we're all in the same boat.

I smiled as I imagined all the people in the church arguing over who was the most important.

Imagine if everyone wanted to bring up the gifts. Or if everyone wanted to be a server.

Or if the servers were envious of the choir and tried to sing louder than the singers did.

Or if the ushers said it wasn't fair that they didn't get to do what Father Joe did.

Or if Father Joe said it wasn't fair that he didn't get to be the pope!

Suddenly I felt very different inside. I was happy that Noah got to carry the cruet because I was sure it made him feel responsible. I was thankful for all the people who did different things at Mass. We couldn't have Mass at all without Father Joe, but everyone doing their part was important.

Each of us should do what you are calling us to do, Jesus, I decided, *without bragging about it and without being envious of other people.*

After all, we are all in the same boat!

Where Is It
in the Bible?

Each Gospel tells the story of Jesus with different details. The Gospels according to Matthew, Mark, and Luke each have a similar story about Jesus calling a child over to be an example for his disciples. Here is the one used as a basis for the story of Rebecca in this book:

Then they came to Capernaum; and when he was in the house he asked [his disciples], "What were you arguing about on the way?" But they were silent, for on the way they had argued with one another who was the greatest. He sat down, called the twelve, and said to them, "Whoever wants to be first must be last of all and servant of all." Then he took a little child and put it among them; and taking it in his arms, he said to them, "Whoever welcomes one such child in my name welcomes me, and whoever welcomes me welcomes not me but the one who sent me" (Mark 9:33–37).

In the story, Rebecca and her family live in Gennesaret. This village is mentioned in both the Gospel according to Mark and the Gospel according to Matthew. Here is what it says in Matthew:

When they had crossed over, they came to land at Gennesaret. After the people of that place recognized him, they sent word throughout the region and brought all who were sick to him, and begged him that they might touch even the fringe of his cloak; and all who touched it were healed (Matthew 14:34–36).

Here's the Gospel story about the storm at sea that Caleb heard at Mass. As you read it, imagine what it was like to be in that storm and then for Jesus to quiet it:

On that day, when evening had come, he said to [his disciples], "Let us go across to the other side." And leaving the crowd behind, they took him with them in the boat, just as he was. Other boats were with him. A great windstorm arose, and the waves beat into the boat, so that the boat was already being swamped. But he was in the stern, asleep on the cushion; and they woke him up and said to him, "Teacher, do you not care that we are perishing?" He woke up and rebuked the wind, and said to the sea, "Peace! Be still!" Then the wind ceased, and there was a dead calm. He said to them, "Why are you afraid? Have you still no faith?" And they were filled with great awe and said to one another, "Who then is this, that even the wind and the sea obey him?" (Mark 4:35–41)

Written by Maria Grace Dateno, FSP
Illustrated by Paul Cunningham

Three ordinary kids, six extraordinary adventures, one incredible quest!

Join Caleb, Hannah, and Noah as they're whisked away to the time of Jesus and find themselves immersed in some of the most amazing Bible stories of all!

Also available: Mystery of the Missing Jars (#4), Courageous Quest (#5), and Discovery at Dawn (#6)

Who are the Daughters of St. Paul?

We are Catholic sisters. Our mission is to be like Saint Paul and tell everyone about Jesus! There are so many ways for people to communicate with each other. We want to use all of them so everyone will know how much God loves us. We do this by printing books (you're holding one!), making radio shows, singing, helping people at our bookstores, using the internet, and in many other ways.

Visit our Web site at www.pauline.org

BOOKS & MEDIA

The Daughters of St. Paul operate book and media centers at the following addresses. Visit, call or write the one nearest you today, or find us at www.pauline.org.

CALIFORNIA

3908 Sepulveda Blvd, Culver City, CA 90230	310-397-8676
935 Brewster Avenue, Redwood City, CA 94063	650-369-4230
5945 Balboa Avenue, San Diego, CA 92111	858-565-9181

FLORIDA

145 S.W. 107th Avenue, Miami, FL 33174	305-559-6715

HAWAII

1143 Bishop Street, Honolulu, HI 96813	808-521-2731

ILLINOIS

172 North Michigan Avenue, Chicago, IL 60601	312-346-4228

LOUISIANA

4403 Veterans Memorial Blvd, Metairie, LA 70006	504-887-7631

MASSACHUSETTS

885 Providence Hwy, Dedham, MA 02026	781-326-5385

MISSOURI

9804 Watson Road, St. Louis, MO 63126	314-965-3512

NEW YORK

64 W. 38th Street, New York, NY 10018	212-754-1110

SOUTH CAROLINA

243 King Street, Charleston, SC 29401	843-577-0175

TEXAS

Currently no book center; for parish exhibits or outreach evangelization, contact: 210-569-0500, or SanAntonio@paulinemedia.com, or P.O. Box 761416, San Antonio, TX 78245

VIRGINIA

1025 King Street, Alexandria, VA 22314	703-549-3806

CANADA

3022 Dufferin Street, Toronto, ON M6B 3T5	416-781-9131